Usborne Spotter's Guides

TREES

Esmond Harris
Director of the Royal Forestry Society

Illustrated by Annabel Milne & Peter Stebbing

Additional illustrations by Aziz Khan

Edited by Jane Chisholm, Ingrid Selberg and Sue Jacquemier
Designed by Nickey Butler and Andrea Slane
Cover designer: Michael Hill
Series designer: Laura Fearn
Series editor: Philippa Wingate
with thanks to Zoë Wray and Lucy Parris
Consultant: Derek Patch, Director, Tree Advice Trust
Acknowledgements: Cover © Corbis (Royalty-Free); 1 © Richard Hamilton Smith/Corbis;
2-3 © Digital Vision; backgrounds 4-57 and 60-63 © Digital Vision;
58-59 © James Marshall/Corbis

CONTENTS

4 How to use this book
6 The leaves
8 Flowers and fruits
10 Finding the right tree
12 What else to look for?
14 Conifers
32 Broadleaved trees
58 Identifying winter buds
60 Scorecard
62 Internet links
64 Index

HOW TO USE THIS BOOK

This book is an identification guide to some of the trees of Britain and Europe. Take it with you when you go out spotting. Not all the trees will be common in your area, but you may be able to find many of them in large gardens and parks.

WHAT TO LOOK FOR

There are lots of clues to help you identify a tree - whatever the time of year.

Yew

Oak

Common beech

In spring and summer, look at the leaves and flowers. In autumn, look out for fruits, and in winter examine twigs, buds, bark and tree shape.

CONIFER OR BROADLEAF?

The trees in this book are divided into two main groups: conifers and broadleaves.

Conifers have narrow, needle-like or scaly leaves, and their fruits are usuallly woody cones. Most conifers are evergreen, which means they keep their leaves in winter. Their shape is more regular than broadleaved trees.

Sitka Spruce

Broadleaved trees have broad, flat leaves and seeds enclosed in fruits, such as nuts. Most are deciduous, which means they lose their leaves in autumn.

English Elm

Throughout this book, you will find suggested links to tree websites. For a complete list of links and instructions, turn to pages 62-63.

KEEPING A RECORD

Next to each picture and description is a small blank circle.

Whenever you spot a new tree, put a tick in the circle to remind you what you have seen.

This is an example of how the trees are shown.

Circle for ticking

Leaf

Fruits

Flower

10m
Height of tree
in metres

Bark

⬆ CRAB APPLE

Small, rounded leaves with toothed edges. Pinkish-white flowers in May. Small, speckled reddish-green apples.

THE SCORECARD

Use the scorecard at the back of the book to give yourself a score for each tree you spot. A common tree scores 5 points and a very rare one is worth 25 points. If you like, you can add up your score after a day out spotting.

TREE	Score	Date spotted
Aleppo pine	25	5/7/06
Aspen	15	20/7/06
Atlas cedar	10	26/7/06

Fill in the scorecard like this.

THE LEAVES

Leaves will often give you the biggest clue to the identity of a tree. Be careful, though, because some trees have very similar leaves. There are many different types of leaves. Here are some of the most common ones.

Oval (Copper beech)

Narrow (Crack willow)

Triangular (Poplar)

SIMPLE LEAVES

A leaf that is in one piece is called a simple leaf. Simple leaves can be many shapes: round, oval, triangular, heart-shaped, or long and narrow. The edges are sometimes spiky (like holly) or toothed (slightly jagged). Some leaves have very wavy edges, called lobes.

Spiky (Holly)

Lobed (Oak)

Lobe

Heart-shaped (Lime)

6

COMPOUND LEAVES

A leaf that is made up of smaller leaves, or leaflets, is called a compound leaf.

Finger-like
(Horse chestnut)

Leaflets

Feather-like
(Common ash)

CONIFER LEAVES

Many conifers have narrow, needle-like leaves – either single, in small bunches, or in clusters. They can be very sharp and spiky. Some conifers, such as cypresses, have tiny scale-like leaves, which overlap one another.

Bunch of needles
(Atlas cedar)

Pair of long needles
(Corsican pine)

Short single needles
(Norway spruce)

Scale-like leaves covering twigs
(Lawson cypress)

7

FLOWERS AND FRUITS

All trees produce flowers that later develop into fruits, though some flowers are so small you can hardly see them. Most flowers have both male and female parts, but a few species, such as holly, have male and female flowers on separate trees.

Crab apple blossom

Hazel - catkins

Tulip tree flower

FRUITS AND SEEDS

Fruits contain the seeds that can grow into new trees. Broadleaved trees have many different kinds of fruits and seeds. Here are some of them.

Crack willow flowers

Winged fruits (Maple)

Downy seeds (Willow)

Acorn (Oak)

Seed pods (False acacia)

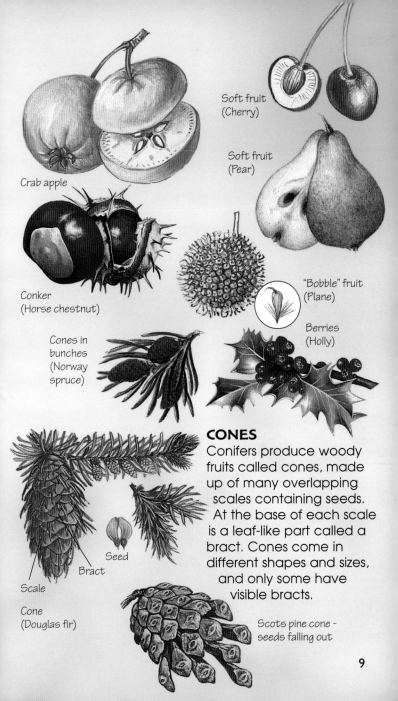

Soft fruit
(Cherry)

Soft fruit
(Pear)

Crab apple

Conker
(Horse chestnut)

"Bobble" fruit
(Plane)

Cones in
bunches
(Norway
spruce)

Berries
(Holly)

Seed

Bract

Scale

Cone
(Douglas fir)

CONES

Conifers produce woody
fruits called cones, made
up of many overlapping
scales containing seeds.
At the base of each scale
is a leaf-like part called a
bract. Cones come in
different shapes and sizes,
and only some have
visible bracts.

Scots pine cone -
seeds falling out

FINDING THE RIGHT TREE

The trees in this book are divided into conifers and broadleaves, with more closely related trees - such as all the oaks - grouped roughly together.

   If you spot a tree you can't identify - but you know what type of leaf it has - you can use this chart to help you match it up with a tree in this book. The numbers show you where you'll find the illustration.

BROADLEAVES
Simple

Unlobed leaves

Common alder	36	Silver birch	40
Common beech	43	Common pear	44
Southern beech	42	Holly	54
Crab apple	44	Aspen	38
Holm oak	33	Western Balsam poplar	39
Whitebeam	37	Goat willow	41
Black Italian poplar	38	White willow	42
Lombardy poplar	40	Silver lime	48
Crack willow	41	Wych elm	49
Common lime	48	Wild cherry	51
English elm	49	Black mulberry	52
Sweet chestnut	50	Cork oak	34
Bird cherry	51	Blackthorn	45
Grey alder	36	Magnolia	57
Hornbeam	43		

Lobed leaves

English oak	32	Sessile oak	32
Red oak	34	Turkey oak	33
White poplar	39	London plane	46
Sycamore	46	Norway maple	47
Field maple	47	Tulip tree	56
Maidenhair tree	56	Hawthorn	45

Compound
Leaves with a central stem

Common ash	35
Rowan	37
False acacia	53
Manna ash	35
Common walnut	52
Tree of Heaven	57

Finger-like

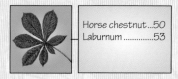

Horse chestnut	50
Laburnum	53

CONIFERS

Single needles

Norway spruce	18	Grand fir	22
European silver fir	20	Douglas fir	23
Noble fir	22	Juniper	27
Western hemlock	23	Coast redwood	29
Yew	28	Greek fir	21
Sitka spruce	18	Spanish fir	21

Needles grouped in 2s

Scots pine	14
Maritime pine	14
Stone pine	15
Corsican pine	16
Shore pine	15

Needles grouped in 3s

Monterey pine	17

Needles grouped in 5s

Swiss stone pine	17

Needles in more than 5s - Evergreen

Atlas cedar	30
Cedar of Lebanon	30
Deodar cedar	31

Needles in more than 5s - Deciduous

European larch	19
Japanese larch	19

Other conifers

Swamp cypress	26
Dawn redwood	28

Scale-like leaves

Nootka cypress	20	Western red cedar	24
Lawson cypress	24	Italian cypress	25
Monterey cypress	25	Leyland cypress	26
Japanese red cedar	27	Wellingtonia	29
Chile pine	31		

For links to websites with tree identification guides, turn to page 62.

WHAT ELSE TO LOOK FOR?

Although the most obvious way to identify a tree is by its leaves, there are lots of other features to look out for too.

TREE SHAPE

You can sometimes tell a tree by its shape, especially in winter when many trees are bare. The leafy top of a tree is called its crown, and each type of tree has its own particular crown shape. This comes from the arrangement of its branches.

Cone-shaped
(Norway spruce)

Narrow crown
(Lombardy poplar)

Broad crown
(Oak)

TWIGS

Look closely at the way the leaves are arranged on the twigs. On some trees, they grow opposite each other in matching pairs. On other trees, the leaves are single and alternate from one side of the twig to the other.

The leaves of a Silver birch alternate from one side of the twig to the other.

The leaves of a Horse chestnut grow opposite each other in pairs.

12

For links to sites about the different parts of a tree, turn to page 62.

BARK

The outside of a tree is covered in a hard, tough layer of bark, which protects the tree from drying out and from damage by insects and other animals. The type of bark a tree has can give clues to its identity too.

Silver birch peels off in wispy strips that look like ribbons.

The bark of Scots pine flakes off in large pieces.

English oak has deep ridges and cracks.

Beech has smooth thin bark, which flakes off in tiny pieces.

On the right is a cross-section of a tree trunk, showing the different layers, or rings. Each year, the trunk thickens by growing a new layer.

CONIFERS

⬇ SCOTS PINE

Short, blue-green, needles in pairs, and small pointed buds. The bark is red at the top of the tree, and grey and furrowed below. The young tree has a pointed shape, becoming flat-topped with age.

Small bud

Short needles in pairs 5-7cm

Green, pointed cone turns brown in second year

The bark flakes off in "plates"

Long bare trunk is red near top of tree

35m

⬇ MARITIME PINE

Long, stout, grey-green needles in pairs; long spindle-shaped buds; and long, shiny brown cones grouped in clusters. Rugged bark on a long, bare trunk.

Long needles in pairs 15-20cm

Cones stay on tree for several years

Long bud

22m

14

Green cones
turn brown
with age

Paired
needles
12-15cm

⬆ STONE PINE
Umbrella-shaped tree
with a flat top, found
on the Mediterranean
coast. Long dark-green,
paired needles, small
buds, and broad cones
with edible seeds.

20m

Young
shoot

Prickly
scales

Paired
needles
4-5cm

23m

⬆ SHORE PINE
Tall, narrow, fast-growing,
with small cones in clusters.
Yellow-green needles in pairs
on twisted shoots, scaly bark,
and sticky, bullet-shaped buds.

15

For a link to a website with a tree-designing game, turn to page 63.

CONIFERS

Branches grow at regular intervals

36m

⬆ CORSICAN PINE
Tall, fast-growing Mediterranean tree, found on rocky hillsides. Long, dark-green, paired needles; onion-shaped buds; and large lop-sided brown cones. Blackish bark.

Paired needles 12-18cm

Cones take two years to ripen

Young shoot

Paired needles

Shiny, reddish cones stay on tree for many years

Rare in Britain

10m

⬆ ALEPPO PINE
Small, round-topped Mediterranean tree, with bright-green, paired needles and small round buds. Its cones usually come in groups of two or three.

16

Lower branches sometimes touch the ground

Found in the Alps and other mountainous areas

Needles in fives
7-9cm

Bark is rugged and scaly

17m

↑ SWISS STONE PINE

Small, cone-shaped tree, with dense, stiff needles that come in fives. Small, pointed, sticky buds and egg-shaped cones, with edible seeds that ripen and fall in their third year.

↓ MONTEREY PINE

Slender, grass-green needles in threes. Large, pointed, sticky buds and squat cones growing flat against the branches, staying on the tree for many years.

Needles in threes - about 10cm

Large, pointed sticky buds

Cones uneven at base

30m

CONIFERS

Needles
1-2cm

Cone scales are
tightly closed

↑ NORWAY SPRUCE
Traditional Christmas tree.
Regular conical shape, with
prickly dark-green needles,
and cones which hang
down. Leaves peg-like
bumps on the twigs when
the needles are pulled off.

30m

Cones have
papery scales
with crinkled
edges

Needles
2-3cm

35m

Grey, scaly bark
flakes off in "plates"

↑ SITKA SPRUCE
Narrow cone-shaped
tree, with prickly blue-
green needles and fat
yellow buds. Small knobs
left on yellow twigs when
needles are pulled off.

18

For a link to a website about growing Christmas trees, turn to page 62.

Fine, feathery branches

38m

↑ EUROPEAN LARCH
Bunches of soft, light-green needles, which turn yellow and fall in winter, leaving small barrel-like knobs on twigs. Small, egg-shaped cones and reddish female flowers.

Straw-coloured twigs

Bare tree in winter

↓ JAPANESE LARCH
Bunches of blue-green needles, which fall in winter, leaving orange twigs. Pinkish-green female flowers and small, flower-like cones.

Edges of scales turn backwards

The tree has thick branches

35m

Bare tree in winter

19

CONIFERS

Young cones are green, turning plum-coloured with age

25m

⬆ NOOTKA CYPRESS
Fern-like sprays of dull green, scale-like leaves grow on either side of the twigs. Plum-coloured cones have prickles on their scales. Cone-shaped crown.

⬇ EUROPEAN SILVER FIR
Flat single needles, green above and silvery below. Flat, round scars left on twigs when needles drop. Cones shed their scales when ripe, leaving a brown spike.

Large, upright cones

Bracts showing

Rare in Britain, but common in central Europe

Very tall, narrow tree

40m

The twigs are smooth and the needles have notched tips

30m

The needles have pointed tips

Bark flakes off in "plates"

⬆ GREEK FIR

Shiny green, spiny-tipped needles all around twig. Tall, narrow cones shed scales to leave bare spikes on tree. Found only in parks in Britain.

⬇ SPANISH FIR

Short, blunt, blue-grey needles all around twig. Cylindrical, upright cones, which shed scales when ripe, like the European silver fir.

The needles have blunt tips

The tree has a conical shape

28m

21

For links to sites where you can solve tree mysteries, turn to page 62.

CONIFERS

The needles are shorter at the top of the twig

40m

Bracts do not show

↑ GRAND FIR
Tall tree, with dark, shiny green needles, arranged like the teeth of a comb, fragrant when crushed. Whitish buds and small, upright cones.

↓ NOBLE FIR
Level branches and dense silver-blue needles, curving up. Enormous shaggy cones with down-turned bracts. Scales fall off, leaving tall spikes.

Bract

Cones up to 20cm long

Flat-topped crown

37m

For a link to a website about tree record-breakers, turn to page 63.

↑ DOUGLAS FIR

Soft, scented needles, copper-brown buds with long points, and light-brown hanging cones with three-pointed bracts. Its bark is thick and grooved when old.

40m

Bract

↓ WESTERN HEMLOCK

Smooth, brown scaly bark, drooping branch tips and top shoots with small cones. Needles of various lengths, green above and silver below.

Tips of branches droop

Older cones are brown

Flattened needles

Young cones are green

35m

23

CONIFERS

⬇ WESTERN RED CEDAR

Small, flower-shaped cones and smooth, finely furrowed bark. The twigs are covered with flattened sprays of scented, scale-like leaves.

Open cone

Leaves are dark, shiny green above and streaked white below

30m

⬇ LAWSON CYPRESS

Sprays of fine, scale-like leaves, green and other colours. Small, round cones and smooth, reddish bark. The leader shoot (at tree top) often droops.

Small cones

Spray of scale-like leaves

25m

Cones are shiny pale-green at first, dull grey when older

↓ ITALIAN CYPRESS

An upright, narrow crowned, mainly ornamental tree. Small, dark, dull-green, scale-like leaves, closely pressed to stem. Large, rounded cones.

Leaves are smaller than Monterey cypress (below)

15m

↓ MONTEREY CYPRESS

Dense sprays of small, scale-like leaves and large, purplish-brown, rounded cones with knobs on scales. Column-shaped, becoming flat-topped when old, and the bark is often peeling.

Leaves are lemon-scented when crushed

Peeling bark

25m

Knob

CONIFERS

Triangular-shaped crown

Tree in winter

The leaves are not dense

Cone

20m

↑ SWAMP CYPRESS

Soft, feathery, light-green needles that appear late and drop in winter, leaving orange twigs. Reddish-brown spiralled bark, often peeling. Round, purplish-brown cones.

↓ LEYLAND CYPRESS

Sprays of dense, bright-green, scale-like leaves. Rare, round grey-brown cones. Thick, column shape, often seen as a hedge.

Lower branches touch the ground

Reddish-brown furrowed bark

20m

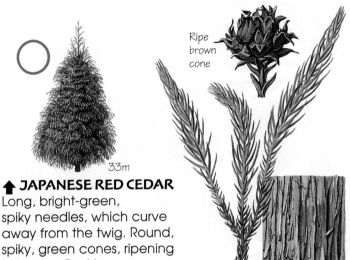

Ripe brown cone

⬆ JAPANESE RED CEDAR
Long, bright-green, spiky needles, which curve away from the twig. Round, spiky, green cones, ripening to brown. Red-brown peeling bark.

33m

The fruits look like berries

Sharp needles in threes

Needles smell strongly when crushed

⬇ JUNIPER
Often found as a shrub. Sharp blue-green needles in threes around shoot, with a white band on the upper surface. Berry-like fruit, turning purplish-black in second year.

20m

27

CONIFERS

Wide, spreading branches

15m

↑YEW

Seen in churchyards, as a wide, spreading tree or as a hedge. Red, berry-like fruit and wide needles, dark-green above and yellowish below. Orange-brown flaking bark.

Leaves and berries are poisonous

The cones are on long stalks, but rare

⬇ DAWN REDWOOD

Soft, light-green needles, similar to the Swamp cypress (see page 26), but larger, turning reddish in autumn. Bark is orange in young trees, flaking and furrowed in older ones.

The needles turn reddish in autumn

Bare tree in winter

20m

Needles parted
on either side
of the twig

COAST REDWOOD

Tall tree, with thick,
reddish, spongy bark.
Hard, sharp-pointed,
single needles, dark-
green above and
white-banded
below. Small,
round cones.

33m

WELLINGTONIA

Tall, with soft, thick, deeply
furrowed bark. Deep-green,
scale-like, pointed leaves,
hanging from upswept
branches. Long-stalked,
round, corky cones.

Diamond-shaped
cone scales wrinkle
when they ripen

Foliage hanging
from upswept
branches

38m

CONIFERS

⬇ ATLAS CEDAR

Large, spreading tree
with dark-green needles,
in bunches on the older
shoots. Large, barrel-
shaped, upright cones
with sunken tops.

Sunken top

Leaves are
blue-green in
the common
garden variety,
dark green in
the wild

25m

Top not
sunken

Cones are
covered with
sticky resin

30m

⬆ CEDAR OF LEBANON

Similar to Atlas Cedar, but
without sunken tops on
cones. Level branches with
masses of table-like leaves.

Leaves overlap
each other

↓ CHILE PINE
Strange-looking tree, with
twisting branches, wrinkled
bark, and a pole-like trunk.
Stiff, leathery, triangular
leaves with sharp points
grow all around
the shoots.

Broad,
round
crown

23m

↓ DEODAR CEDAR
A tall cedar, with a pointed
crown and soft, pale-green
leaves, in bunches.
Large, barrel-
shaped cones.

The top shoot
and branch
tips droop

23m

31

For a link to a website about the secret life of trees, turn to page 63.

BROADLEAVED TREES

Tall acorns on long stalks

Acorn cup

Lobe

⬆ ENGLISH OAK
Broad-crowned tree with many large branches growing upwards from the same point. Leaves are short-stalked with ear-like lobes at the base.

23m

⬇ SESSILE OAK
Thick, dark, long-stalked leaves tapering to the base. Branches grow from stem at different levels and point up in a narrow crown.

All veins go to tips of lobes

Acorn more rounded than English oak

Acorn is often stalkless

21m

⬇ HOLM OAK

Ornamental tree with
a broad dense crown.
Shiny, evergreen leaves,
greyish-green beneath,
sometimes with shallow
teeth like Holly.

Teeth

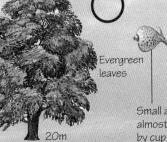

Evergreen
leaves

20m

Small acorn,
almost covered
by cup

⬇ TURKEY OAK

Leaves unevenly lobed.
Whiskers on buds and at
base of leaves. Acorns
ripen in second autumn.
Acorn cups mossy and
stalkless.

Acorn cup
is mossy

25m

33

For a link to a site about a year in the life of a tree, turn to page 62.

BROADLEAVED TREES

Cork is obtained
from the bark

Twisted trunk
and branches

16m

Acorn

↑ CORK OAK
Common in southern
Europe, but extremely
rare in Britain. Smaller
than other oaks, it has
thick, corky, whitish bark
and shiny, evergreen
leaves with wavy edges.

↓ RED OAK
Smooth, silvery bark, and
squat acorns in shallow
cups that ripen in second
year. Large leaves, with
bristly-tipped lobes, turn
reddish brown in autumn.

The leaves turn
reddish in
autumn

Acorn

20m

34

For a link to a website about leaf change in autumn, turn to page 62.

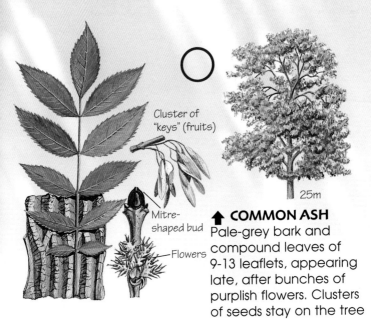

Cluster of "keys" (fruits)

Mitre-shaped bud

Flowers

25m

↑ COMMON ASH

Pale-grey bark and compound leaves of 9-13 leaflets, appearing late, after bunches of purplish flowers. Clusters of seeds stay on the tree into winter.

↓ MANNA ASH

Smooth grey bark oozing a sugary liquid called manna. Leaves of 5-9 stalked leaflets appear with clusters of white flowers in May.

Fruit

Flowers

Leaflets downy near veins

20m

35

BROADLEAVED TREES

Leaf has
notched tip

12m

Ripe brown,
woody cone

↑ COMMON ALDER
Rounded leaves fall in
late autumn, reddish
catkins and small, brown,
woody cones. Sticky
young twigs and leaves.
Often found near water.

↓ GREY ALDER
Fast-growing, with catkins
and fruit like the Common
alder. Pointed oval leaves,
with sharply-toothed,
edges, soft and grey
beneath.

These green fruits
ripen into brown,
woody "cones"

14m

One flower
(from a
cluster)

Leaves with
toothed
edges

7m

Leaves turn red
in the autumn

↑ ROWAN

Often grows alone on
mountainsides; also known
as Mountain Ash. Tooth-
edged compound leaves,
smaller than other ashes.
Clusters of creamy-white
flowers in May, and red
berries in August.

↓ WHITEBEAM

Flowers and berries similar
to Rowan, but ripening
later. Large oval leaves,
with toothed edges, dark-
green above, white and
furry underneath.

Berries

8m

BROADLEAVED TREES

Leaf stalks are long and flattened

⬆ ASPEN
Rounded leaves with wavy edges, deep-green on top, paler beneath. White downy catkins. Grey bark with large irregular markings. Often found growing in thickets.

20m

Tree in winter

⬇ BLACK ITALIAN POPLAR
Dark-green, triangular, pointed leaves appearing late. Red catkins and deeply furrowed bark. Trunk and crown often lean away from the wind.

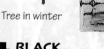

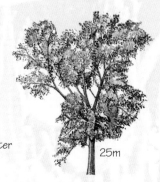

Tree in winter

25m

Lower leaves are less lobed

Wavy
edges

Underside of leaf

Diamond-
shaped marks
on young bark

↑ WHITE POPLAR
Five-lobed leaves, downy
white underneath, so the
crown looks white. Lower
bark is dark and rugged;
upper bark, pale grey,
with diamond shapes on
young trees. Tree often
leans slightly.

20m

↓ WESTERN BALSAM POPLAR
Large, triangular, pointed
leaves, very pale
underneath. Sticky and
sweet-smelling buds
and young
leaves. Long
purplish catkins
and white
fluffy seeds.

35m

Underside of leaf

39

BROADLEAVED TREES

Leaf shape varies
slightly

28m

↑ LOMBARDY POPLAR
Tall, narrow tree, often
found along roadsides on
the European continent.
Pointed, triangular leaves,
furrowed bark, and
branches that grow
upwards from the ground.

15m

↑ SILVER BIRCH
Slender tree with silvery
bark and drooping
branches. Small,
diamond-shaped leaves,
with toothed edges, and
long "lamb's tail" catkins,
in April.

Catkin

Silvery bark
peels off
in ribbons

↑ GOAT WILLOW

Broad, rounded, rough, grey-green leaves. Silvery-grey upright catkins, known as "pussy willow", in late winter. Small bushy tree. Common on damp waste ground.

7m

Catkin "Pussy willow"

Underside of leaf

The crown shape varies

Broad crown

15m

↑ CRACK WILLOW

Grows near water and often has its branches cut back to the trunk. Leaves very long and narrow, bright-green above and grey-green below. Its twigs are easy to snap off.

Underside of leaf

Catkin

BROADLEAVED TREES

Underside of leaf

Catkin

↑ WHITE WILLOW
Found by streams and rivers. Long, narrow, finely toothed leaves, white underneath. Slender twigs that are hard to break. One variety with trailing branches is known as Weeping willow.

20m

Leaves on short stalks

Fruits

20m

↑ SOUTHERN BEECH
Triangular-shaped crown, and narrow, oval leaves, with fine-toothed edges and many obvious veins. Deep-green, prickly fruit, and silver-grey bark.

Leaves are
wavy-edged

Husk

Nuts

25m

↑ COMMON BEECH
Tall tree with a spreading
crown. Light-green, oval
leaves that turn copper
brown in autumn. Smooth
grey bark, and triangular
nuts with hairy husks.

10m

↑ HORNBEAM
Sharply-toothed, oval
leaves. In autumn, clusters
of three-pronged, leaf-like
wings hold nuts. Smooth,
grey bark is fluted, or rippled.

Cluster
of green
winged
fruits

43

BROADLEAVED TREES

⬇ CRAB APPLE

Small, bushy tree, found in hedges. Small, rounded leaves with toothed edges. Pinkish-white flowers in May. Small, sour, speckled reddish-green apples that can be used in cooking.

Apple tastes sour even when ripe

10m

⬇ COMMON PEAR

Found in woods and hedgerows. Large, white flowers in April. Small pears that are gritty to eat. Small, dark-green leaves, with finely toothed edges and long stalks.

Pear is golden when ripe

15m

↑ BLACKTHORN

5m

Small tree, with oval leaves; foamy, white flowers on bare twigs in March; and small, blue-black fruit, called sloes, in September.

Berries called haws

↑ HAWTHORN

8m

Shiny, deeply lobed, dark-green leaves and thorny twigs. Clusters of small, white flowers in May, and dark-red berries. Rounded crown.

For a link to a website about how trees make food, turn to page 62.

BROADLEAVED TREES

⬆ LONDON PLANE
Large, broad leaves in pairs, with pointed lobes. Spiny "bobble" fruits hang all winter. Flaking bark, leaving yellowish patches. Often found in towns.

30m

Fruit

Leaves have toothed edges

Fruits twist as they fall

⬆ SYCAMORE
Large spreading tree, with dark-green leathery leaves with toothed edges and five lobes. Paired, right-angled, winged fruits. Smooth brown bark, becoming scaly.

20m

For links to interactive tours of virtual forests, turn to page 63.

15m

↑ NORWAY MAPLE
Light-green, thin leaves, with bristle-tipped lobes and teeth. Wide-angled, paired fruits and finely furrowed, grey bark.

Pairs of fruits spin as they fall

Lobes are blunt

Leaves turn golden in autumn

10m

↑ FIELD MAPLE
Small, round-headed tree, often found in hedges. Small, dark-green leaves with five lobes, and small, reddish, winged fruits.

Fruits

47

BROADLEAVED TREES

Broad crown

25m

↑ **COMMON LIME**
Heart-shaped leaves
with toothed edges.
Yellowish-green,
scented flowers in July.
Small, round, hard,
grey-green fruits hang
from a leafy wing.

Leafy
wing

Fruits

Pointed tip

↓ **SILVER LIME**
Like the Common lime,
but with a more rounded
crown. Dark-green leaves,
silvery-grey below. Fruits
hang from a leafy wing.

Leafy
wing

Fruits

Rounded
crown

20m

For a link to a website about making leaf rubbings, turn to page 63.

Tall, narrow crown
often has uneven shape

Now
rare in
Britain

Flowers

Uneven base

30m

Fruit

Short
point

⬆ ENGLISH ELM

Rough, oval leaves
with double-toothed
edges and uneven
bases. Clusters of red
flowers appear before
leaves.

⬇ WYCH ELM

Like the English elm,
but with a round, even
crown; larger, rougher,
stalkless leaves; and
larger seeds. Now very
rare in Britain.

Uneven
base

Fruit

Clusters
of red
flowers

20m

BROADLEAVED TREES

⬇ HORSE CHESTNUT

Brown, inedible "conkers" in green, spiny cases. Compound leaves of 5-7 large leaflets. "Candles" of white or pink flowers in May.

Upright "candle" of flowers

Leaflet

Tree in bloom

25m

Conker (seed)

⬇ SWEET CHESTNUT

Clusters of edible brown chestnuts in prickly cases. Long, narrow leaves with saw-toothed edges. Bark sometimes spiral-furrowed.

Male flowers

Female flower

20m

Leaves turn
red in autumn

↓ WILD CHERRY
White blossom in April and
red, edible (though sour)
cherries. Large, pointed,
oval leaves with toothed
edges. Reddish-brown
bark peels in ribbons.

Red
cherries
contain
single
stones

Upper branches
grow upwards

Horizontal marks
on shiny bark

Lower
branches level

15m

↓ BIRD CHERRY
Leathery, finely toothed,
oval leaves, followed by
drooping spikes of small
white flowers. Small black
cherries attract birds.

Spike of flowers

Leaves
turn
pale
yellow in
autumn

Tree is
sometimes
bushy

Cherry

Bark is
not shiny

13m

51

BROADLEAVED TREES

Unripe fruit

Ripe fruit

Young fruits

⬆ BLACK MULBERRY
Rough, heart-shaped
leaves with toothed edges.
Blackish-red berries. Short
trunk, twisted branches.
Flowers in short spikes.

25m

Smooth, green case
containing edible walnut

Young
fruit

⬇ COMMON WALNUT
Broad crown. Smooth, grey
bark, with some cracks.
Compound leaves of
seven to nine leaflets,
and hollow twigs.

Leaves are
bronze when
they first
open,
turning
green later

20m

Smooth-edged leaflet

20m

↑ FALSE ACACIA

Smooth-edged compound leaves of many small leaflets. Hanging clusters of white flowers in June. Seeds in pods. Pairs of sharp thorns on twigs. Often has several trunks.

Deeply furrowed bark

↓ LABURNUM

Leaf made up of three leaflets. Hanging clusters of yellow flowers. Poisonous seeds in twisted brown pods. Smooth green-brown bark.

Leaflets are soft and hairy

Young seed-pods are green

Tree in bloom (May-June)

7m

BROADLEAVED TREES

⬇ HOLLY

Small tree with shiny, dark, evergreen leaves with thorny prickles. Small, white flowers. Round red berries. Smooth grey-green bark.

Leaves are thick and leathery

Berries appear only on the female trees

10m

Male flower

Female flower

Flowers

Leaves

Tree in bloom   3m

⬆ TAMARISK

Tiny, grey-green, scale-like leaves, which look feathery. Clusters of small pinkish-white flowers. Shrub or small tree with slender branches. Often found near the sea.

Twig

For a link to movie clips about planting trees, turn to page 63.

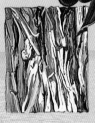

(Not in Britain)

10m

Edible fruits
are oily with
hard stones

○

↑ COMMON OLIVE

Small Mediterranean tree
with a twisted trunk and
narrow evergreen leaves
in pairs. Clusters of small
whitish flowers. Fleshy
green fruit ripens to black.

↓ EUROPEAN
FAN PALM

Large, fan-shaped leaves
made up of 12-15 stiff,
pointed parts. Large
clusters of small flowers
and fruits. In the wild, it
forms trunkless clumps
of leaves.

Rare in
Britain

○

Tall trunk
only in
planted
trees

4m

Hairy
trunk

55

BROADLEAVED TREES

Squared lobe

Cone-like fruit

⬆ TULIP TREE
Smooth, four-lobed leaves, golden in autumn. Large tulip-like flowers in June. Upright, brown, cone-like fruits.

20m

Flower

Cleft

⬇ MAIDENHAIR TREE
Tall, slender tree. Double-lobed, fan-shaped leaves with deep cleft, bright yellow in autumn. Female trees have hanging fruit, but male trees are more common.

Maidenhair tree is neither a conifer nor a broadleaved tree. It is in a group on its own.

Fruit looks like a small plum

23m

↑ MAGNOLIA

Wide, spreading tree.
Large white flowers on
naked twigs in March,
before large, smooth,
dark-green, oval leaves.

10m

Winged fruits ripen from
green to reddish-brown

Smooth grey-brown
bark with white streaks

22m

↑ TREE OF HEAVEN

Large compound leaves
made up of 5-20 pairs of
stalked leaflets. Large
clusters of greenish flowers
in July, followed by clusters
of winged fruits.

IDENTIFYING WINTER BUDS

Most broadleaved trees have no leaves in winter, but you can often identify them by their winter buds. These contain the beginnings of next year's shoot, leaves and flowers.

What shape is the twig? What colour are the buds, and are they pointed or rounded? Are they positioned in opposite pairs, or single and alternate? Is the bud covered with hairs or scales? If scales, how many are there? Is the bud sticky?

False acacia

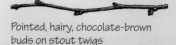

Small buds with thorns at base, on grey, crooked, ribbed twigs

English elm

Pointed, hairy, chocolate-brown buds on stout twigs

Ash

Large, black opposite buds on silver-grey twigs

Turkey oak

Clusters of small, brown, whiskered, alternate buds

Common alder

Alternate, stalked purple buds, often with male catkins

For links to websites with lots of fun tree activities, turn to page 63.

White poplar

Small, orange-brown buds covered by white, felty hairs on green twigs

Sweet chestnut

Rounded, reddish-brown buds on knobbly, greenish-brown twigs

Common beech

Long, pointed, copper-brown buds sticking out from brown twigs

London plane

Alternate, brown cone-shaped buds with ring scars around them

Sycamore

Large green, opposite buds, with dark-edged scales on stout, light-brown twigs

Common walnut

Big, black, velvety triangle-shaped, alternate buds on thick, hollow twigs

Whitebeam

Downy, green, alternate buds

White willow

Slender buds enclosed in a single scale, close to pinkish, downy twigs

Common lime

Zigzag twig. Alternate, reddish buds with two scales

Wild cherry

Fat, shiny, red-brown buds grouped at the tips of light brown twigs

SCORECARD

The trees on this scorecard are arranged in alphabetical order. Fill in the date on which you spot a tree beside its name. A common tree scores 5 points, and a rare one is worth 25. After a day's spotting, add up all the points you have scored on a sheet of paper and keep a record of them. Can you score more points another day?

TREE	Score	Date spotted	TREE	Score	Date spotted
Aleppo pine	25		Corsican pine	10	
Aspen	15		Crab apple	10	
Atlas cedar	10		Crack willow	10	
Bird cherry	10		Dawn redwood	25	
Black Italian polar	10		Deodar cedar	5	
Black mulberry	25		Douglas fir	10	
Blackthorn	5		English elm	15	
Cedar of Lebanon	10		English oak	5	
Chile pine	10		European fan palm	25	
Coast redwood	20		European larch	10	
Common alder	5		European silver fir	15	
Common ash	5		False acacia	10	
Common beech	5		Field maple	15	
Common lime	10		Goat willow	5	
Common olive	25		Grand fir	15	
Common pear	20		Greek fir	20	
Common walnut	15		Grey alder	15	
Cork oak	25		Hawthorn	5	

TREE	Score	Date spotted	TREE	Score	Date spotted
Holly	5		Sessile oak	10	
Holm oak	10		Shore pine	10	
Hornbeam	10		Silver birch	5	
Horse chestnut	5		Silver lime	20	
Italian cypress	20		Sitka spruce	10	
Japanese larch	15		Southern beech	20	
Japanese red cedar	15		Spanish fir	20	
Juniper	15		Stone pine	25	
Laburnum	5		Swamp cypress	25	
Lawson cypress	5		Sweet chestnut	10	
Leyland cypress	5		Swiss stone pine	25	
Lombardy poplar	10		Sycamore	5	
London plane	5		Tamarisk	15	
Maidenhair tree	20		Tree of Heaven	20	
Magnolia	15		Tulip tree	20	
Manna ash	20		Turkey oak	10	
Maritime pine	15		Wellingtonia	10	
Monterey cypress	15		Western balsam poplar	10	
Monterey pine	15		Western hemlock	10	
Noble fir	10		White poplar	10	
Nootka cypress	20		White willow	5	
Norway maple	5		Whitebeam	10	
Norway spruce	5		Wild cherry	5	
Red oak	10		Wych elm	15	
Rowan	5		Yew	5	
Scots pine	5				

INTERNET LINKS

If you have access to the Internet, you can visit these websites to find out more about trees. For links to these sites, go to the Usborne Quicklinks Website at **www.usborne-quicklinks.com** and enter the keywords "spotters trees".

Internet safety

When using the Internet, please follow the **Internet safety guidelines** shown on the Usborne Quicklinks Website.

IDENTIFYING TREES

WEBSITE 1 A guide to help you identify trees.

WEBSITE 2 A tree identification guide and guess-the-tree games.

WEBSITE 3 A detailed online guide to trees.

WEBSITE 4 A tree and shrub identification guide.

HOW TREES GROW

WEBSITE 1 A close-up look at tree rings.

WEBSITE 2 Let Pierre Acorn show you why trees are terrific on an interactive tour of the different parts of a tree.

WEBSITE 3 Find out how trees and plants make their own food, then solve a tree mystery.

WEBSITE 4 An animated, interactive class at Dr. Arbor's tree school.

WEBSITE 5 Follow a year in the life of a tree, see the different forms a tree can take and discover how useful trees really are.

WEBSITE 6 Find out how Christmas trees are grown, harvested and recycled.

WEBSITE 7 An animation explaining why leaves change colour in autumn.

WEBSITE 8 Discover the secret life of trees as Pierre Acorn shows you what goes on inside a tree.

WEBSITE 9 Design your own tree, and find out how it would cope in different climates.

WEBSITE 10 Investigate the trees and plants in a virtual garden to find out about the effects of climate change.

WOODLAND LIFE

WEBSITE 1 Take a walk in a virtual wood and find out about woodlands and woodland life.

WEBSITE 2 Watch movie clips about tree planting and woodland wildlife, play a cyber tree game and discover why woodlands are important.

WEBSITE 3 Go for virtual expeditions into a forest to carry out investigations into the life of trees.

WEBSITE 4 Explore a conifer woodland and discover the plants and animals that live there.

FUN TREE ACTIVITIES

WEBSITE 1 Fun, online tree activities plus lots of information about tree planting.

WEBSITE 2 Find out all about what makes a tree a tree then try out some tree activities.

WEBSITE 3 A game to build a tree ring timeline.

WEBSITE 4 How to make leaf rubbings.

WEBSITE 5 Try to save a badger wood its animals.

INDEX

Aleppo pine, 16
Aspen, 38
Atlas cedar, 30

Bird cherry, 51
Black Italian poplar, 38
Black mulberry, 52
Blackthorn, 45

Cedar of Lebanon, 30
Chile pine, 31
Coast redwood, 29
Common alder, 36
Common ash, 35
Common beech, 43
Common lime, 48
Common olive, 55
Common pear, 44
Common walnut, 52
Cork oak, 34
Corsican pine, 16
Crab apple, 44
Crack willow, 41

Dawn redwood, 28
Deodar cedar, 31
Douglas fir, 23

English elm, 49
English oak, 32
European fan palm, 55
European larch, 19
European silver fir, 20

False acacia, 53
Field maple, 47

Goat willow, 41
Grand fir, 22
Greek fir, 21
Grey alder, 36

Hawthorn, 45
Holly, 54
Holm oak, 33
Hornbeam, 43
Horse chestnut, 50

Italian cypress, 25

Japanese larch, 19
Japanese red cedar, 27
Juniper, 27

Laburnum, 53
Lawson cypress, 24
Leyland cypress, 26
Lombardy poplar, 40
London plane, 46

Magnolia, 57
Maidenhair tree, 56
Manna ash, 35
Maritime pine, 14
Monterey cypress, 25
Monterey pine, 17

Noble fir, 22
Nootka cypress, 20
Norway maple, 47
Norway spruce, 18

Red oak, 34
Rowan, 37

Scots pine, 14
Sessile oak, 32
Shore pine, 15
Silver birch, 40
Silver lime, 48
Sitka spruce, 18
Southern beech, 42
Spanish fir, 21
Stone pine, 15
Swamp cypress, 26
Sweet chestnut, 50
Swiss stone pine, 17
Sycamore, 46

Tamarisk, 54
Tree of Heaven, 57
Tulip tree, 56
Turkey oak, 33

Wellingtonia, 29
Western balsam poplar, 39
Western hemlock, 23
Western red cedar, 24
White poplar, 39
White willow, 42
Whitebeam, 37
Wild cherry, 51
Wych elm, 49

Yew, 28